ideals®
COUNTRY

Publisher, Patricia A. Pingry
Editor, Nancy J. Skarmeas
Art Director, Patrick McRae
Editorial Assistant, LaNita Kirby

ISBN 0-8249-1091-5

IDEALS—Vol. 48, No. 4 June MCMXCI IDEALS (ISSN 0019-137X) is published eight times a year: February, March, May, June, August, September, November, December by IDEALS PUBLISHING CORPORATION. P.O. Box 148000, Nashville, Tenn. 37214. Second-class postage paid at Nashville, Tennessee, and additional mailing offices. Copyright © MCMXCI by IDEALS PUBLISHING CORPORATION. POSTMASTER: Send address changes to Ideals, Post Office Box 148000, Nashville, Tenn. 37214-8000. All rights reserved. Title IDEALS registered U.S. Patent Office.

SINGLE ISSUE—$4.95
ONE-YEAR SUBSCRIPTION—eight consecutive issues as published—$19.95
TWO-YEAR SUBSCRIPTION—sixteen consecutive issues as published—$35.95
Outside U.S.A., add $6.00 per subscription year for postage and handling.

BRIGHT MEADOWS by Grace Noll Crowell: From the book THE CRYSTAL FOUNTAIN by Grace Noll Crowell. Copyright © 1948 by Harper & Brothers. Reprinted by permission of HarperCollinsPublishers. Excerpts from MY COUNTRY by Russell W. Davenport: Used by permission of Natalie P. Davenport. PROUD FATHER by Edgar A. Guest: Used by permission of the estate. THE COUNTRY STORE by William F. Hunt: Used by permission of the estate. OUR BEAUTIFUL LAND by Bessie Trull Law: Used by permission of the estate. OLD STONE MILL by Maxine Lyga, from the book POEMS FROM THE HILL: Used by permission. THE SAME THINGS OVER by Douglas Malloch: Used by permission of the estate. FARM MEMORIES by Violet Bigelow Rourke: Used by permission of the estate. ONE GOLDEN GIFT by Garnett Ann Schultz from the book MOMENTS OF SUNSHINE: Copyrighted—used by permission of the author. THE MESSAGE OF THE FLOWERS by Myrtie Fisher Seaverns, from the book HILLS OF HOME. © 1948 by Helen Seaverns Melvin. Used by permission. FOURTH OF JULY CELEBRATIONS from MOMENTS OF ETERNITY and STILLNESS from SPLENDID MOMENTS, by Betty W. Stoffel: Used by the author's permission. STABILITY by Edna Jaques from THE GOLDEN ROAD. Copyright © in Canada by Thomas Allen and Son Limited; BUILDING A NATION by Edna Jaques from MY KITCHEN WINDOW. Copyright © 1935 by Thomas Allen & Son Limited. TO THE NEXT GENERATION by Edna Jaques from PRAIRIE BORN, PRAIRIE BRED. © 1979 in Canada by Western Producer Prairie Books. Used by permission of the estate. Our sincere thanks to the following whose addresses we were unable to locate: Catherine E. Berry for COUNTRY FRAGRANCE; Marie Daeer for PAST JUNES; Marty Hale for EXAMPLE; Ruth Scott Hubbard for MYSTERY OF THE SOIL; Amy Roberts for THE OLD FARMHOUSE; Anton J. Stoffle for I DO NOT TREASURE MAN-MADE THINGS; May Smith White for AN OLD FAMILIAR ROAD.

Four-color separations by Rayson Films, Inc., Waukesha, Wisconsin

Printing by The Banta Company, Menasha, Wisconsin

The paper used in this publication meets the minimum requirements of American National Standard for Information Sciences—Permanence of Paper for Printed Library Materials, ANSI Z39.48-1984.

Unsolicited manuscripts will not be returned without a self-addressed stamped envelope.

Vol. 48 , No. 4

Inside Front Cover
POSTING THE DECLARATION
Francis Chase

Inside Back Cover
THE RETURN OF THE LIBERTY BELL
Francis Chase

Cover Photo
H. Armstrong Roberts

One Golden Gift

Garnett Ann Schultz

God sends to us one golden gift,
It starts with one bright dawn;
The darkness quickly fades to light
And nighttime then is gone.
Enchantment fills our hearts with joy;
We hear the singing birds;
In hush and quietness we wait,
No need for human words.

God wraps the day in one blue sky
Atop the world so bright:
A carpet soft in summer's world,
The green grass of delight.
The rolling hills and singing streams,
A shaded lane of bliss;
As fleecy clouds go floating by—
No thrill is quite like this.

God bids the world to come awake
As sleeping meadows sigh;
Within the laughter of the dawn
We watch a butterfly
And honeybees, buzzing there
Amidst the clover's bloom.
One golden gift—this summer day
With all the world in tune.

Photo Opposite
CRAFTSBURY, VERMONT
Dietrich Stock Photos

Softly Comes June

Kay Hoffman

Softly comes the month of June
    with roses in her hair;
Pretty flowers in pastel shades
    are blooming everywhere.

The cooing of the mourning dove,
    the butterfly's bright wings,
Songbirds nesting in the trees—
    June brings such lovely things.

The little brook, less boisterous now,
    plays a soft, new tune;
Fleecy clouds on an azure sky
    can't help but chase our gloom.

The countryside so picturesque
    with peaceful meadow scenes—
A place to weave a daisy chain
    and pause awhile to dream.

May with her fairy blossoms
    is queen but for a day;
Then softly comes the month of June
    to steal our hearts away.

ABANDONED ROAD
Cades Cove
Great Smoky Mountains National Park, Tennessee
Adam Jones, Photographer

SUMMER AFTERNOON

Grace V. Watkins

This afternoon the wind and I
Went strolling down the avenue
Beneath a lovely shining sky
Of morning glory blue.

And walking on the sun-bright way
I said a quiet, whispered prayer
Of thanks for every summer day
So gloriously fair!

WAGON WHEEL GATE
Gatlinburg, Tennessee
Adam Jones, Photographer

LET ME REMEMBER

Mabel Jones Gabbott

Let me remember as the days grow long
How brief a time is summer, how sweet her song,
How children take delight in barefoot days,
The garden's joyance in the hot sun's rays,
The full maturing of flower and fruit,
And the garnering of good from leaf and root.

From early freshness through the heat of noon,
To lingering twilight—summer goes too soon.

Summer's Child

I love the red-winged blackbird's songs
When snow-wet land awakes.
I thrill to wild calls of loons
That float on rippled lakes.

I love gold mushrooms after rain,
Young jewelled limbs of leaves
Reflecting sunlight's glowing threads,
The tapestry it weaves.

I sense those yearning flowing threads
That stitch out loops in soil
Or rounding arcs of rainbow mist
A-shimmer on lake's foil.

And I too am the summer's child
With sunlight on my face.
I run barefoot down wet roads
In love with God's glad grace!

Barbara Sherrard Morgan
Brainerd, Minnesota

I Wish

I wish I were an artist
So I could paint the sky;
I'd paint the fluffy white clouds
As they're slowly drifting by.

I'd paint the gorgeous sunrise
That brings another day,
So we may see the beauty
All around us laid.

I'd paint the noonday sun
That burns so hot and bright;
It helps the grass and flowers grow
And that's a beautiful sight.

Then I'd paint the setting sun
As it slowly sinks from sight;
It brings an ending to the day
With a black velvet night.

Esther Williams
Cape Coral, Florida

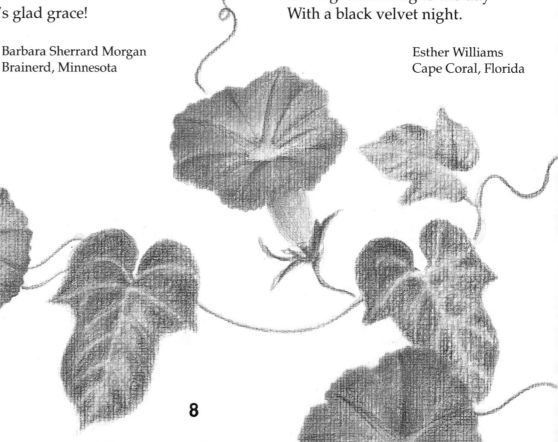

Reflections

Bouquets of Blessing

The world would be a poorer place
Without your flowers, Lord;
I'm glad you used a lavish hand
To toss them on our world.

From dawn to dark they lift
Their cups of perfume toward the sky,
And nod with wanton loveliness
To every passerby.

No vale so deep but what a blossom
Lifts a fragrant face,
No rocky steep too grim but knows
A flower's sturdy grace.

They lend themselves to prim design
In stately garden plan;
They bend themselves in windswept freedom
O'er the meadowland.

They sing a cheery silent song
In sickrooms everywhere;
They pass from loving hand to hand,
And clearly say "I care."

They speak when other tongues are stilled,
And fill my poignant hours
With messages too sweet for words;
O thank you, Lord, for flowers!

E. Ruth Glover
The Dalles, Oregon

Editor's Note: Readers are invited to submit unpublished, original poetry, short anecdotes, and humorous reflections on life for possible publication in future *Ideals* issues. Please send copies only; manuscripts will not be returned. Writers receive $10 for each published submission. Send material to: "Readers' Reflections," Ideals Publishing Corporation, P.O. Box 140300, Nashville, TN 37214-0300.

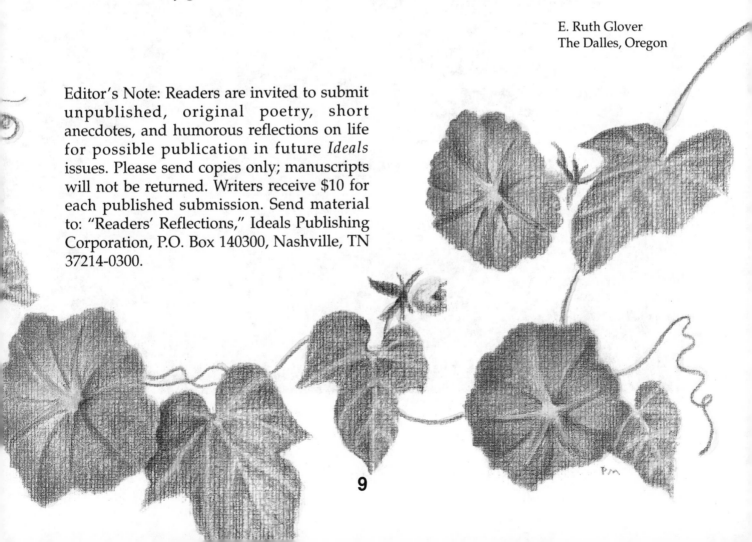

Joys of June

June Masters Bacher

The hedge has grown unruly;
It hides the garden gate.
The figs are still producing,
But peaches will not wait.

The early cukes are ready;
The dill has gone to seed.
Most everything needs water,
And there's no time to weed.

The cabbage heads are bursting;
I should get to the kraut.
Potato bugs need dusting—
That I could do without!

The black-eyed peas need canning;
They've never done so well.
The jelly grapes are early
In clustered purple bells.

Ah, how they scent the arbor
And play a merry tune;
I hum along right with them:
I love the month of June!

GENTLY SUMMER

Alice Mackenzie Swaim

Gently summer reprimands
The bustle of my restless hands.
The sky, like Chinese porcelain,
With blossoms delicate as rain
Surrounds me with serenity
And bolsters my identity.
Tranquility, breast-feather light,
Disguises every sound or sight
That might conspire to do me harm,
Or startle my spirit to alarm,
And casts a wash of rainbow haze
Across the dust of sun-baked days.

Carpe Diem

Mary E. Linton

Then live this hour as though there
    were but one,
This whole bright day as if it were the last.
Remember, heart, the things that you
    wished done,
And grasp this moment ere it, too, is past.

Oh, could we pack such living in a year
As we could manage if that year were all!
Release from life's uncertainty and fear
Would set our spirits free to stand up tall.
And who among us holds a guarantee?
Can we be certain that this is not true?
Then why not be whatever we would be,
Reach out for dreamed-of heights beyond
    the blue!
No time but now—no holding what
    we seek
Except in living each day at its peak.

PHLOX
Gene Ahrens, Photographer

The Message of the Flowers

Myrtie Fisher Seaverns

Sweet blossoms breathe remembrance
Of dear friends of bygone days,
Whose spirits seem yet with us
In the old familiar ways.

Sweet blossoms breathe forgetfulness
Of sorrow, pain, and care,
As their haunting, healing perfume
Sheds its fragrance on the air.

Sweet blossoms breathe a blessing,
On the spirit crushed and sore,
That heals and soothes and comforts,
And renews its hope once more.

Sweet blossoms bring new courage
To the soul in deepest need,
Giving joy and peace and healing—
A priceless gift, indeed.

Sweet blossoms breathe benediction,
A blessing and a prayer,
God's loving message bearing
To his children everywhere.

THE OLD MANSE
Concord, Massachusetts
Dianne Dietrich Leis Photography

TRAVELER'S *Diary*

Remaining Faithful: Iowa's Amana Colonies

Your goal and your way shall lead toward the west to the land still open to you and your faith. I am with you and shall lead you over the sea.

Christian Metz

On July 21, 1842, Christian Metz made this solemn pronouncement to his followers in the German Church of True Inspiration. Church members faced increasing persecution in Germany, and they looked to Metz—a *werkzeuge*, or prophet—for guidance. At his urging, over eight hundred church members headed west across the Atlantic to America, settling in Buffalo, New York. Only twelve years later, Metz directed his people once more, this time to 25,000 acres of virgin farmland in eastern Iowa. Here they settled for good, naming their new home Amana, from the Song of Solomon (4:8), meaning "remain faithful."

And faithful they have been. The seven Amana colonies have flourished, adapting to economic and social change without abandoning the ideals of their ancestors. Once an isolated community, the Amanas now draw thousands of visitors each year with their old-fashioned charm and hospitality. In Amana, travelers find more than a collection of historic artifacts and recreations. The faith that sustained the original settlers is still the foundation of life in the

colonies, and the sense of community that this shared faith inspires is extended to all those who make Amana a part of their travels.

The Church of True Inspiration was founded in the eighteenth century by Eberhard Gruber and Johann Rock, two Lutherans who had become disillusioned by their church's growing emphasis on ritual and tradition. They called for a renewed commitment to personal Bible study and informal devotional meetings. Gruber and Rock believed that God still spoke directly to his people through inspired individuals—the *werkzeuges*—just as he had in biblical times. These prophets, and not church intellectuals, were to serve as guides to the individual in his search for religious meaning.

The True Inspirationalists met with opposition from the Lutheran establishment, an opposition bolstered by their refusal to send their children to Lutheran schools and their unwillingness to perform national military service. Despite the increasing persecution, however, the True Inspirationalists persevered, quietly and patiently, for years. It was not until Christian Metz directed them to look to the west that they decided to seek a new home in America.

Once in Buffalo, church members faced new obstacles. Their emphasis on personal religious experience implied an inherent equality among

18

members; but under the harsh and isolated circumstances of the colony, not everyone was equally successful. Economic pressures threatened the cohesiveness of the group. The solution was the establishment of a communal society in which each woman, man, and child was guaranteed food, shelter, and security in exchange for work on behalf of the common good.

The system worked, even more so once the colony was transplanted to Iowa and its abundant and fertile farmland. For nearly seventy-five years the people of Amana's seven villages thrived. The women cared for children, prepared meals in communal kitchens, and practiced traditional crafts; the men worked in the fields and set up shops as carpenters and blacksmiths and butchers; the children attended community schools. At the center was the Amana church, where community members met eleven times each week for meetings, Bible study, sermons, and prayer.

Life in Amana continued quiet and tranquil until the depression, when economic pressures once again threatened the survival of the group. The simple agricultural way of life that had served the people so well no longer provided sustenance, and young people, for the first time, were tempted to leave the colonies to find work.

Faced with dissolution, Amana adapted. The Great Change of 1932 split the Amana colonies into two branches. The Amana Society, a profit-sharing corporation run by Amana residents, would manage business and farming; the Amana Church Society retained control over church and school matters. Each resident was paid for services rendered under the communal plan and given shares in the new corporation. The official, communal union was dissolved; for the first time, Amana residents owned their land and homes and were responsible for their own financial survival.

But old habits die hard. The people of Amana, accustomed to working together for the common good, continued to do so; and they flourished once more. Communal kitchens became restaurants and bed and breakfasts without sacrificing their commitment to wholesome, friendly service. The small local woolen mill expanded, and soon Amana-made clothing and rugs drew faithful customers from outside the colonies. Amana Refrigeration, a business begun by an enterprising Amana man looking for a way to support his family, grew into one of the world's leading manufacturers of refrigerators and microwaves without altering the peaceful rural environment of the colonies.

Times have changed in Amana. Today, residents are just as likely to make their living working at the refrigeration plant as they are by farming, and church services are generally held one time each week, not eleven. But although times have changed, the community established more than one hundred and fifty years ago remains intact. Travelers come to these villages for their history. They come to tour museums and exhibits that provide a wonderful picture of early American life. They come to buy exquisitely crafted rugs and furniture, and to taste regional specialties like cinnamon bread and German sausage. They come for the beautiful countryside and the relaxed pace of Iowa country life. But what they find is that the historical Amana still exists, not as a preserved relic of a bygone era, but as seven functioning modern villages.

Christian Metz and his followers chose wisely when they named their new settlement so many years ago. The Amana community has been through transplantation, isolation, depression, and industrialization. Each new challenge has been met with the same faithful commitment to church, family, and community that carried the original settlers across the Atlantic. This is the secret to the Amanas' success as a community, and the key to their appeal to travelers. A community confident of its union and proud of its heritage, Amana welcomes outsiders, ready and willing to share its achievement with the world.

Oat and Wheat Bread

1	cup cracked wheat
¼	cup firmly packed brown sugar
2	teaspoons salt
2	cups water
¼	cup molasses
3	tablespoons vegetable oil
2	packages active dry yeast
4¾-5¾	cups flour
1	cup oats
1	egg
1	tablespoon oats

In large bowl, combine cracked wheat, brown sugar, and salt. Heat water to boiling and stir in molasses and oil; add to dry ingredients, mixing well. Set aside; cool to lukewarm (105° to 115°). Dissolve yeast in ⅔ cup lukewarm water. Add to wheat mixture. Stir in 2 cups flour, blending at low speed of mixer until moistened; beat 2 minutes at medium. Add oats and 2¼ to 3¾ cups flour, stirring until dough pulls away from sides of bowl. Turn out on floured surface and knead in remaining ½ to 1 cup flour until dough is smooth and elastic, about 10 minutes. Place dough in lightly greased bowl, turning once to grease top. Cover and let rise in warm place until doubled (45 to 60 minutes).

Punch dough down to remove air bubbles. Divide dough in half and shape into two round loaves. Place on two greased cookie sheets. Slash ¼-inch deep lattice design in tops. Cover and let rise in warm place until doubled (about 1 hour).

Preheat oven to 350°. Brush loaves with beaten egg and sprinkle tops with oats. Bake 25 to 45 minutes or until loaves are golden brown and sound hollow when tapped. Remove from cookie sheets; cool on wire racks.

NUTRITION INFORMATION PER SERVING

Serving size:	1 slice	Percent U.S. RDA per serving:	
Calories	130	Protein	6%
Protein	4g	Vitamin A	*
Carbohydrate	25g	Vitamin C	*
Fat	2g	Thiamine	10%
Cholesterol	8mg	Riboflavin	6%
Sodium	140mg	Niacin	6%
Potassium	7mg	Calcium	*
		Iron	8%

* Contains less than 2% of the U.S. RDA of this nutrient.

Mystery of the Soil

Ruth Scott Hubbard

If I could understand the mystery of the soil,
How sod and air and belabored toil
Could bring to pass in their quiet way
Such grandeur as we see each day
Along furrowed hillsides as we fare,
Haystacks and hanging vines with fruit
    to spare.

If I could understand how bright-hued flowers
Could grace tall stems and garland bowers,
Spread perfume on the midnight air,
And face each surprise without care,
When each beginning was a shriveled bulb
Or dank, dark earth long undisturbed,
I'd have to my account knowledge rich, replete,
Chronicled on God's own ledger sheet.

Stillness

Betty W. Stoffel

There is a stillness in fresh-furrowed fields
At rest before the growing of the grain;
There is a stillness in the tear-emptied sky
That cried for joy in gratifying rain.
There is a stillness in the watchful heart
That daily scans the field and deeply knows
The restiveness of one who plants and waits
For evidence of life in what he grows.

There is a stillness in the harvest heart
At peace before the bounty of his toil,
Matching good of earth with good of sky
In gratitude to God for seed and soil.
There is a stillness in the souls of men
Who watch new miracles of growth each
    year again.

The Same Things Over

Douglas Malloch

The farmer plows the same soil over,
Plants this year's corn on last year's clover,
Walks the new rows
That this year knows,
Where last year's rows are seen no more,
And finds that some new harvest grows
Where some old harvest grew before.

And like the farmer's field is duty:
The oldest task has some new beauty.
At morning's sound
The same old ground
We plow, and walk the same old ways;
But call it not "the same old round"—
Today's task is always today's.

Who drives a spindle, writes a letter,
I know each day can do it better,
Love some task more
Than loved before,
Make some more noble fashioned thing.
Ah, yes, we plow the same soil o'er,
But every morning it is spring!

VEGETABLE GARDEN
Larry Lefever
Grant Heilman Photography

24

Deana Deck

Year-Round Tomatoes

What would summer be without garden-fresh tomatoes?

From the moment I set their fragrant seedlings into the soil until the day their aroma fills the kitchen as I blanch, peel, and can them by the dozen, tomatoes mark the days of summer more accurately than any calendar. Until the soil has warmed enough to satisfy the tender tomato, I know it is not really spring; and only when I can no longer slice into a fresh-picked "Red Chief" still warm from the sun am I convinced summer is truly over.

Here in the South, harvesting can continue long into fall even when logic would dictate that plants should have already succumbed to frost, if not advanced age. In warmer climates, the tomato—a native of Peru that migrated to Mexico where it was discovered by European explorers—can be grown year round. And luckily for tomato lovers in northern climates, container-grown tomatoes can provide a succulent treat even as winter storms are rampaging through the garden.

If large tomatoes are your goal, the best harvests are obtained by planting a mix of early, mid-season, and late varieties. Although somewhat smaller than some standard varieties, the "Early Girl" is one of my favorites because it blooms so early in the season. In our climate it can by counted on to bloom by the end of June. I am impressed by this performance, probably because of my grandfather, whose annual goal was to produce a ripe tomato by the Fourth of July. With the "Early Girl," this is no trick at all.

Another excellent early variety that produces much larger fruit is the "Champion," a perfect example of the tomato of the future. It has been carefully bred to be high in disease resistance and is also very tasty. It matures about ten days later than "Early Girl," but the fruit is about twice as large and is highly flavorful.

"Burpee's Big Boy" is a good example of a widely recommended mid-season variety. It requires a continuous supply of water, but it will reward you with a heavy crop of large fruit.

If early fall frost is not a problem in your area, the late varieties will provide excellent table fare long after others have begun to slow down. One of the prettiest and most flavorful of these is the "Red Chief VNF."

The tomatoes mentioned above are all indeterminate varieties. This means that the vine will grow almost indefinitely if not pinched back; and they will continue to grow, bloom, produce fruit, and ripen until a hard frost finally finishes the season.

Determinate varieties, on the other hand, are those which send up a central growing shoot that produces all its blooms and fruits at about the same time. Harvesttime, however, is short, lasting only a week or ten days in some varieties.

Providing the proper growing conditions for your tomatoes is essential. All varieties like at least six hours of direct sunlight daily and plenty of moisture and fertilizer. They should be fed at planting time with a balanced fertilizer high in phosphorus to encourage fruit development. Feed again when fruit is set, and follow up once or twice a month with additional feedings.

Tomato research has led to the development of small varieties of the plant that can be grown indoors in pots. These are wonderful for apartment dwellers with balconies or large sunny windows who crave fresh tomatoes but lack garden space. They can also offer an interesting change of pace from the usual office plant.

A cherry tomato that does especially well at any time of the year is the "Florida Petite." It will only grow to be about six inches tall and can dwell happily in a four-inch pot on a windowsill. This tomato plant will produce masses of the small but delicious fruit.

The "Florida Basket," bred for hanging pots, bears slightly larger fruit from an attractive plant that tumbles dramatically from its container. For patios or balconies, choose the "Florida Lanai." Plant it in a six- to eight-inch container and it will produce thirty or forty tomatoes slightly larger than the standard cherry tomato.

Because of the restricted root space and the more frequent watering that all container plants require, nutrients quickly wash out of the container. So plan to feed these plants more often than you would if they were in the garden. Commercial soil mixes contain the necessary phosphorus for good plant growth; this makes it unnecessary to feed when you first start the seedlings or set transplants in the pot. Wait two or three weeks, then begin feeding with a liquid 5-10-10 plant food.

And while you are waiting, start looking up tomato recipes!

Deana Deck lives in Nashville, Tennessee, where her garden column is a regular feature in the Tennessean.

To the Next Generation

Edna Jaques

Will they love these dear brown fields
    and call them home, and sing,
And watch the amber dawn come up
    against the gates of spring?
Will they love small wrinkled streams
    and gray old lichened trees;
Love to be home at night, and hold
    small children on their knees?

Will they be glad for yellow wheat
    and purple-misted hills,
Small woven nests against the eaves
    and flaming daffodils,
For tiny petals veined with red,
    the smell of rain-washed earth,
For warm clean rooms where someone sings,
    and cradles by the hearth?

From tired hands we pass to you
    the sickle and the plow;
Leave all these dear old farms we knew
    for you to harvest now.
Pass to our children the rod and staff,
    a trust for years to be;
Leaving to them these brown dear fields
    where we held tenancy.

Photo Overleaf
DAIRY FARM
Near Baraboo, Wisconsin
Dietrich Stock Photos

Sonora Smart Dodd: The Mother of Father's Day

Dianne L. Beetler

O n Mother's Day in 1910, Sonora Louise Dodd went to church. The sermon she heard there stirred her to action.

But it wasn't the contents of the message that inspired her. On the contrary, Mrs. Dodd noticed what the minister had omitted. As he extolled the virtues of motherhood, he failed to make one mention of the value of fathers. This omission angered Mrs. Dodd. Fathers, she was sure, deserved equal credit.

Sonora was born in Jenny Lind, Arkansas, in 1882. When she was five, her parents, William and Ellen Smart, joined other pioneers seeking a better life in the West. They settled near Spokane, Washington.

When Sonora was only sixteen years old, her mother died, leaving six children in the care of Mr. Smart. As the oldest, Sonora recognized the magnitude of the task confronting her father, and she tried to do her part in caring for her five brothers and sisters. She watched her father work and sacrifice to raise his children, and for the rest of her life she remembered his courage and devotion. Fathers deserved a special day, too, Sonora decided as she sat in church that Mother's Day. And she would be the one to finally do something about it!

Sonora, who was by this time married and the mother of a small son, approached her minister with the idea of a day for fathers. With his encouragement, she appeared before the Spokane Ministerial Alliance to present her idea. She suggested that fathers be honored on June 5—her own father's birthday.

The Ministerial Alliance was pleased with the idea, but they felt ministers would not have enough time to prepare special sermons if the day were celebrated on June 5. They decided instead to designate the third Sunday in June as their Father's Day.

A local newspaper publicized the new holiday, and store owners used their windows to display appropriate gifts for fathers. On June 19, 1910, Spokane's first Father's Day, young men from the YMCA wore roses to church. A red rose honored a living father; a white rose was worn in memory of a deceased father. Mrs. Dodd herself rode through town in a horse-drawn carriage and distributed gifts to shut-in fathers.

Newspapers across the nation heard about Spokane's Father's Day and promoted the idea. William Jennings Bryan became one of the first nationally known figures to endorse the day; others soon followed his lead. In 1916, President Wilson spoke at Father's Day services in Spokane; and by the time William Smart passed away in 1919 the day his daughter had founded in his honor was celebrated throughout the United States.

Although the American people immediately began to recognize Spokane's Father's Day, Congress was hesitant to make it official. Letters were written, resolutions were presented, and speeches were made; but for years Congress resisted proclaiming Father's Day as a national holiday. Their fear was that such a proclamation would lead to over-commercialization.

Sonora herself did not fear the commercialization of the holiday; she believed that publicity was the only means of ensuring that the American people would remember their fathers and pay tribute to their service, at least one day each year. In 1966—fifty-six years after that Mother's Day morning in church—Sonora wrote the last of a long line of letters to President Johnson and Senator Russell Long, urging them both to support a resolution elevating Father's Day to the same national status as Mother's Day. In 1971, the resolution passed.

Sonora Dodd died in 1978 at the age of ninety-six. She had lived a long and full life, gaining recognition for her art and her writing, including a series of children's books on the Native Americans of Spokane. And through it all she had remained devoted to the memory of her father. Sonora gave sixty-eight years of her life to the cause of honoring William Smart for his sacrifice and his service to his six motherless children. By honoring her father, however, Sonora had reached beyond the limits of her own family and had given fathers everywhere the respect and tribute they deserved.

In the years since 1910 Father's Day has grown from a city-wide observance to a worldwide holiday. Today, more than thirty countries reserve a special day each year for their fathers.

And each one of those fathers owes a special "thank you" to Sonora Smart Dodd—the mother of Father's Day.

Child's Play

Painting by Donald Zolan

Example

Marty Hale

I want my boy to have a dog,
Or maybe two or three.
He'll learn from them much easier
Than he would learn from me;
A dog will show him how to love,
And bear no grudge or hate—
I'm not so good at that myself,
But dogs will do it straight.

I want my boy to have a dog
To be his pal, and friend;
So he may learn that friendship sticks,
Faithful to the end.
And if I should select a school
To teach my boy to live,
I'd get a pair of pups for him
That had these things to give.

There never yet has been a dog
Who learned to double-cross,
Nor catered to you when you won
Then dropped you when you lost.
To teach my boy of friendship's worth
I'll never sign him up
With any school that ever was—
I'll just buy him a pup.

Proud Father

There's a smile on the face of the mother today,
The furrows of pain have been scattered away,
Her eyes tell a story of wondrous delight
As she looks at the baby who came through the night.
It's plain she's as happy and proud as can be,
　　but you ought to see me!

The nurse wears her cap in its jauntiest style,
And she says: "My dear, there's a baby worthwhile!
She's the pink of perfection, as sweet as a rose,
And I never have seen such a cute little nose."
Were it proper for nurses she'd dance in her glee,
　　but you ought to see me!

Bud's eyes are ablaze with the glory of joy,
And he has forgotten he'd asked for a boy.
He stands by her crib and touches her cheek
And would bring all the kids on the street for a peek.
Oh, the pride in his bearing is something to see,
　　but you ought to see me!

You may guess that the heart of the mother is glad,
But for arrogant happiness gaze on the dad.
For the marvelous strut and the swagger of pride,
For the pomp of conceit and the smile satisfied,
For joy that's expressed in the highest degree,
　　take a good look at me!

Edgar A. Guest began his illustrious career in 1895 at the age of fourteen when his work first appeared in the Detroit Free Press. *His column was syndicated in over 300 newspapers, and he became known as "The Poet of the People."*

STABILITY

Edna Jaques

The solid fundamental things of earth
That never change no matter what the age:
Buck brush and willows by a shiny pond,
A summer morning and the smell of sage;

Old fashioned virtues, that we often see:
Clear-minded men and women fine and strong,
A young boy happy in his chosen work
Starting a summer morning with a song;

Hitching a brown team to a walking plow,
Plowing the field as to the manor born,
Rejoicing at the sight of greening fields
And golden tassels forming on the corn;

A couple, middle-aged, yet finding still
The dear companionship of younger days,
A lantern hanging in a dingy barn
Making a golden circle with its rays;

A sturdy cottage on a village street,
A church door open to the passer-by,
A mother leading home a tired child,
A blue star glowing in a twilight sky;

These are the things of piety and worth
That hold together all of God's earth.

HURD HOUSE
Woodbury, Connecticut
Fred M. Dole Productions

COUNTRY FRAGRANCE

Catherine E. Berry

The fragrance of the early morning hours
Drifts in the window while I knead the bread.
The black earth, newly turned, a wisp of smoke,
The scent of grass on which rose petals spread
Designs of pink confetti—these things take
Me back through years of mornings when June came
With jeweled footsteps, garlands in her hair,
And touched the earth with golden, perfumed flame.

If time and circumstance should take me far
From this green, fragrant land, each year I'd know
The same sweet-bitter pain within my heart
When June had set the countryside aglow.
A vase of flowers in a florist shop
Would—for a moment—hold a country lane
Deep bordered, red and pink and white—and I
Could close my eyes and walk it once again!

PAST JUNES

Marie Daerr

Past Junes have a way of coming back, disguised
Ingeniously. A fragile-petaled rose
Transports me to a porch where dusk surprised
The rocking chairs. A wide-winged night moth goes
Up the gray trellis. Mother lifts her shawl,
A ghost thing, from the railing, nestles it
About her throat against the first damp. Words fall
Into the yard where firefly lamps are lit,
Melt into silence and are gently gone.

Then, as the breeze walks leaf trails overhead,
The dog moves shadowed on the cool soft lawn,
Father sends pipe smoke toward the lily bed
And dark treads purposefully down the street,
Sure that its welcome will be soft and sweet.

39

The Country Store

William F. Hunt

I know city stores are very neat,
    in fact, I think they're fine,
With their new-fangled fixtures,
    and their clerks arrayed in line;
And with their bright new wares
    displayed so tidily about,
It tempts you much to purchase—
    of this there is no doubt.

But there is one thing that's missing
    from these stores, I'm sad to say;
That old-time hospitality
    seems somehow gone astray.
Of course, you're greeted with a smile,
    and eagerly they serve,
But from your personal interests
    they are bound to swerve.

How different are the country stores;
    the owner always greets you
With a warm and hearty hand-clasp,
    and a pleasant "Howdy-do?"
"How's all the folks and neighbors?"
    "How's crops?"—"We do need rain."
"Well I'll be, here's Jimmy—
    and here comes Susan Jane."

Somehow you feel you're welcome
    in every country store;
They are never there too busy
    to talk life's problems o'er.
But custom ever changes;
    city business of today
Is strictly classed as business,
    and there's nothing else to say.

THE COUNTRY STORE
Centerville, Cape Cod, Massachusetts
Dick Smith, Photographer

COLLECTOR'S CORNER

Cookie Cutters

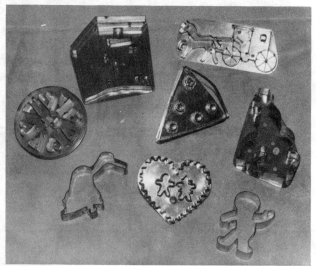

Photos provided by Ruth Capper of the Cookie Cutter Collectors' Club, Dellroy, Ohio.

Just the mention of the word "cookie" fills our minds with images of warm kitchens and the wonderful aroma of homemade treats baking in the oven. Perhaps these associations are part of the reason cookie cutters have become such a popular collectible; after all, who does not like to be reminded of the days when freshly baked cookies and cold milk were waiting on the table after school?

Cookies originated in Rome around the third century B.C. Small wafers were baked twice to reduce their moisture content and thus extend their shelf life. These hard and brittle wafers were named *craken* because of the sound they made when broken. Sweeteners were not added to *craken* until after the Middle Ages. The word "cookie" probably comes from Holland. The Dutch made a small, sweet wedding cake called *koekje*, the diminutive of *koek*, for cake. The *koekje* was softer and more moist than the *craken*.

The origin of the cookie cutter is uncertain, but the first cutters were probably fashioned in simple squares or circles. Made from scrap pieces of tin, the first cookie cutters were likely devised primarily for utilitarian purposes. As cookies became more common, tinkers began to experiment with new shapes and designs.

Throughout our country's early history, cookie cutters were handmade. Many of the examples prior to the late 1800s are in museums or collections. The best indicator of a cutter's age is the width of the cutting strip. The earliest examples were wider, often with crude and spotty soldering. By the late nineteenth century, cutters were mass-produced by factories and sold for pennies in stores and through mail-order houses. The soldering on these later cutters was generally smooth and uniform.

The shape of the backplate is another indication of a cutter's date of origin. Earlier examples have backs that follow the shape of the cutter,

42

there is a club for cookie cutter collectors, and at least one book is devoted entirely to the subject.

Collectors often display cookie cutters in the kitchen—in groupings as wall displays or piled together with a wooden rolling pin on an old breadboard. Many collectibles are made only for viewing. Cookie cutters, however, can be an exception. Put to their original use, cookie cutters have the power to bring a smile to the face of the child—or adult—who tastes the sweetness of a specially shaped cookie, and also to help us make our own, new memories of warm kitchens and the wonderful aromas of home.

while those produced later have round, rectangular, or oval backs.

Collectors must be careful, however, because tinsmiths today can virtually duplicate any cutter. While these cookie cutter replicas have their place as collectibles, collectors should be aware of the true age of any cutter purchased.

Many collectors develop a theme for their collection, buying only those of a certain style or shape. Some collect only handmade cutters, while others look for those made by machine. Cutters have been made in almost every shape imaginable. The more popular shapes are flowers, hearts, gingerbread men, fish, and other animals; but such unusual designs as a slice of cheese and a buzzard are not unheard of. For the most part, the more complicated the design, the higher the price of the cookie cutter.

There are several sources of information for the cookie cutter collector. Besides general information found in books on kitchen collectibles,

Carol Shaw Johnston, a public school teacher, writes articles and short stories. She lives with her family in Brentwood, Tennessee.

43

The Old Stone Mill

Maxine Lyga

The old stone mill with the water wheel
    is still, as if it were dead,
And those who pass by on their journey to town
    think of poems and stories they've read
Of the old water mill by the turn in the bend,
    on the stream, I remember it still,
Where farmers brought wheat to grind into flour
    by the stone of the old grist mill.

It seems there's a dream from out of the past,
    an echo of long, long ago
When the old water wheel by the side of the wall
    tossed the waters to and fro.
Yet the old grist mill is tumbling away,
    though its churning it seems I still hear.
And to those who remember old-fashioned ways
    it's a memory to always hold dear.

Photo Opposite
THE OLD MILL
Gene Ahrens, Photographer

50 YEARS AGO

More Acres for the Lord

Erskine Caldwell had some fun with the idea of *God's Little Acres*: a sly farmer kept moving his consecrated piece of ground to the weediest locations, to make sure that God took a loss instead of a profit. But in the rural South and Midwest the Lord's Acre Plan has saved so many churches that its director last week scheduled a nine-state lecture tour this fall to spread the idea in the Southeast.

Biggest problem in rural church finance is that farmers have little cash to put in the collection plate. But farmers usually have plenty of cotton, wheat, or corn-on-the-hoof—and most of them can be induced to work a few extra hours to raise a bit more to help the church. The Lord's Acre Plan asks churchgoing farmers to till an acre or so, or raise extra livestock, and give the extra cash to the church.

Inspired by the ancient tithe (gift of a tenth), the Lord's Acre Plan got its start outside the churches eleven years ago when James G. K. McClure, pious president of the Farmers Federation of North Carolina and the son of the late theologian James Gore King McClure, decided the federation should have a religion department—something unique for a run-of-the-mill agricultural cooperative. Its project number one was the Lord's Acre Plan, and its head was and is McClure's brother-in-law, the Rev. Dumont Clarke, onetime Presbyterian missionary and

prep school chaplain (Lawrenceville, Andover).

Over a thousand churches of twenty denominations in some twenty states have found financial salvation through the Plan. To Asheville, N.C., Lord's Acre's headquarters, churches in forty-seven states have written for advice. Many a group of missionaries on furlough has flocked to talk with the founders. An important visitor was Japan's No. 1 Christian, Toyohiko Kagawa. Lord's Acres now flourishes in India, China, Brazil, Mexico, and Japan, furnishing rupees, dollars, milreis, pesos, and yen for the local missions.

A Lord's Acre project may be as modest as a pig—North Carolinian Betty Mae Cope raised one for her Methodist church, netted $15.50—or as big as the planting done by farmers near Hendersonville, North Carolina, who ran up a whole new $8,000 Baptist church with their tithing. Hendersonville's Baptists raised $2,352 in a single year by the Plan. Men fattened pigs for market or planted extra crops. The men's bible class grew potatoes as a class project and made $469. Women gave the "Sunday eggs" from their flocks, grew flowers to sell. Children fed chicks until they were fryers, picked berries on the hillside and sold them in town.

There is nothing Caldwellesque about such farms. So proud of them are their owners that the Lord's Acre, often dedicated with a religious service, usually bears a neat sign setting it apart. In fact, there are two North Carolina farms whose enthusiastic owners have named them for the Plan: Lord's Acre Farm No. 1, Lord's Acre Farm No. 2.

FARM MEMORIES

Violet Bigelow Rourke

A brown and white calf named Suzie,
    The creak of an old porch swing,
Gathering eggs from the hen house—
    What joy these memories bring.

Climbing trees in the orchard,
    Pulling buckets up from the well,
Sliding the hay in the old, red barn,
    The clang of the dinner bell;

Bringing the cows from the pasture,
    Picking apples, grapes, and corn,
That first taste of homemade ice cream,
    The rooster crowing at dawn;

Playing with calico kittens,
    So plump with warm, fresh milk,
Hugging the lambs and the puppies,
    Chestnut colts as sleek as silk;

Sniffing the kitchen fragrance
    Of strudels, biscuits, and pies,
The rides in the old farm wagon—
    From the hill, sunset skies;

The duck pond rippling by moonlight
    When katydids and crickets call,
The peace and quiet of evening,
    A rose-strewn cobblestone wall;

These glimpses of childhood adventures
    When my spirit ever roamed free
Sustain and soothe me all my days
    Bringing wonderful memories to me.

Photo Opposite
THE WOOLSEY FARM
Eden Prairie, Minnesota
Bob Firth/Firth Photobank

CHRONICLE

Lansing Christman

I can always find comfort and friendliness in the mountains and the hills that lie deep in the corridors of the land out here in the country.

I find cheer in the songs of the birds, in the babble of the bubbling waters of the brook, in the whisper of the wind, in the nourishment of the rain, and in the warmth of the sun pressed like the palm of a caring hand against my face.

Here in June I look upon the broad sweep of the fields of timothy, where daisies, hawkweed, and St. John's wort wear their colorful corsages of orange, yellow, and white.

I walk along hand and hand with June, looking and listening, touched by the loveliness of it all. Barn swallows swoop and sweep overhead, chattering in their flights to and from the barn. The bobolinks sing their rollicking song as they

alight on timothy stalks, which bend and sway as they are touched. The goldfinch adds its sweet song as it makes its dipping flights over the land; and from somewhere in the pasture, beyond the stone wall, the field sparrow cries plaintively, tugging at the strings of my heart. Blended together, the songs fill the hills with lilting melodies.

Adding to the delight of the country at this time of year are the aromas, like the scent of ripening strawberries in the fields, or the lovely aroma of a wild rose on the stony slope of the pasture. In the evening, it is the common primrose in the old meadow that fills the cooling air with its fragrance.

The country becomes more precious to me with every flower, with every song, and with every year. The outdoor world is a sanctuary of peace and contentment. I stand reverently before the wonders of creation; I feel the presence of God in these wonders, as old as the hills—old, but still always new to me. They are inspiring, like a refreshing dawn on a morning in June.

The author of two published books, Lansing Christman has been contributing to Ideals *for almost twenty years. Mr. Christman has also been published in several American, foreign, and braille anthologies. He lives in rural South Carolina.*

CRAFTWORKS

BRAIDED RAG RUGS

Charlotte Young

Materials Needed:

Fabric scraps
Scissors
Straight pins
Needle and heavy thread

Choosing the Fabric

Rag rugs are made from scraps of fabric, sheets, draperies, or clothing—whatever you have on hand. Most fabrics will make a good rug, but heavy cotton is the best choice. It is important that all the fabric used in a single rug be of similar weight so that the braids will be uniform in size and thickness. Rugs can be made in bands of alternating color, like the one pictured here, or they can be done in a single color. A "tabby" pattern—with colors braided at random—is a good choice if you are using scraps from various sources. The amount of fabric needed depends upon the size rug you choose to make and the weight of your fabric. For the 45-inch rug pictured here, the equivalent of two large sheets will provide more than enough fabric.

Preparing the Fabric

Cut or tear your fabric into long two- to three-inch strips, tapering the last four inches of both ends of each strip to half-width. There is no minimum length of strip required, but the longer the strip, the less extra sewing will be involved. When all fabric has been cut or torn, place the strips on a flat surface. Fold each strip twice lengthwise, right side facing out, so that the two unfinished edges meet in the middle. Next, repeat the two lengthwise folds, this time bringing the two folded edges to meet in the center of the strip, producing a strip ½- to ¾- inch wide. Fold a few inches at a time, rolling the folded strip as you go and securing occasionally with straight pins.

Braiding the Strips

Choose three strips of fabric with which to begin. Rag rugs are braided from the center outward, so the strips you choose, braided together, will form the middle of your rug. Sew these first three strips together, one on top of the other, along the short edge and begin braiding with the strip to your right. Lay this strip over the center strip; it becomes the new center. Next, lay the left strip over the center, making it the new center strip. Continue, right over center; left over center, for the remainder of the braid. Always pull braided strips horizontally away from the braid, never down, to ensure a tight braid.

When you come to the end of a strip, join a new strip by sewing along the four-inch tapered edges. To create more definite color breaks, braid each colored section separately.

Forming the Rug

In order to gauge the size of the rug, and to keep to your color pattern, it is necessary to attach the braid into a rug as you go. This is done by forming a spiral around the end point and stitching the braid to itself along the outer edges, always keeping it flat. If you are working with one continuous strip, continue braiding a section and stitching a section until the rug is the desired size and pattern. Make sure that the last four inches of the final three strips braided taper for a smooth finish. If your rug is made up of separately braided strips, attach each as above, adding new sections by overlapping the tapered ends to maintain a braid of equal thickness.

Photo Opposite
Gerald Koser

Simple Summer Pleasures

Cynthia McFarland

It's here. Official. The long, lazy days of summer have arrived.

Actually, one has to wonder about the "lazy" part. It seems that summer is brimming with things to do and places to go. Perhaps "lazy" refers to the luxury of simply being able to choose what, when, and where.

There are a number of pleasures that are strictly for summer; they are reminders that the season is truly here. During the heat of the day, I enjoy the civilization of an air conditioner, but in the evenings and early mornings, the windows are open. It is soothing to hear the murmur of wind chimes on my porch, to see the curtains dance in the breeze, and to hear the birdsong. After dark, the soft night sounds join together in a goodnight chorus—the calling of the whippoorwill, the chirping of the crickets in the grass, and the low, throaty voices of frogs after a rain.

The fields about my home are flecked with the delicate faces of Queen Anne's lace. A generous bunch of the flowers arranged in a favorite vase brings summer into my kitchen.

Often late into the evening, tractors are at work in a nearby hay field. It is oddly comforting to hear the motor's sound and to see them steadily moving across that open expanse, silhouetted against the setting sun as the dusk begins to settle. I don't envy the long, dusty hours of labor; but there is a sense of security somehow in knowing that as long as there is summer, they will be there—cutting, raking, fluffing, bailing—sending the sweet scent of freshly cut alfalfa drifting on the breeze.

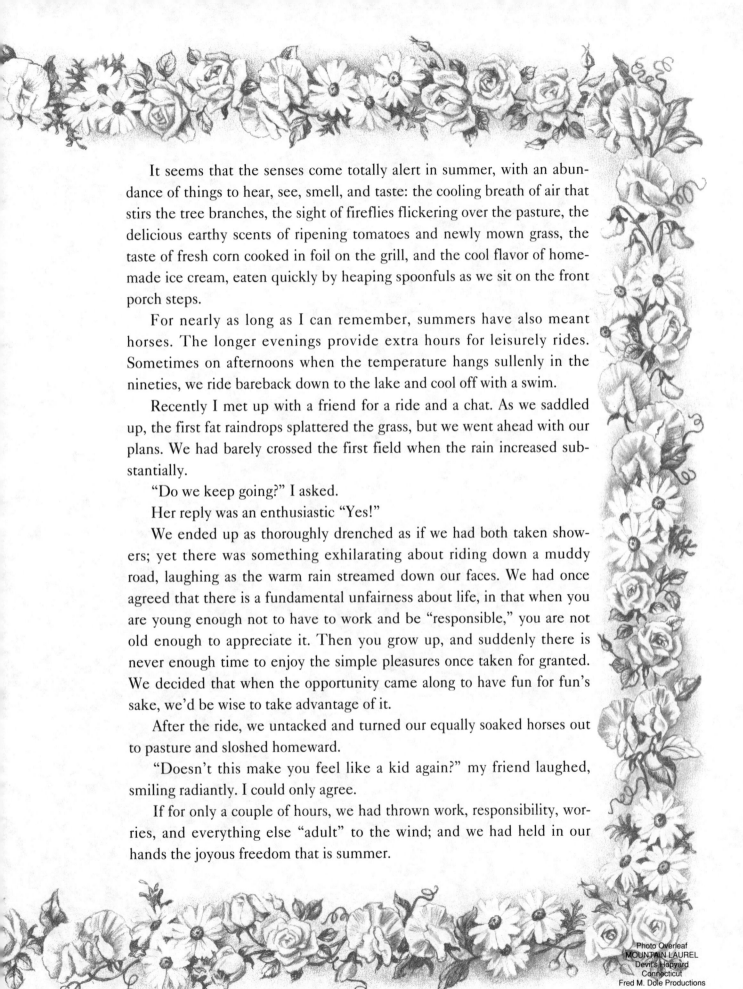

It seems that the senses come totally alert in summer, with an abundance of things to hear, see, smell, and taste: the cooling breath of air that stirs the tree branches, the sight of fireflies flickering over the pasture, the delicious earthy scents of ripening tomatoes and newly mown grass, the taste of fresh corn cooked in foil on the grill, and the cool flavor of homemade ice cream, eaten quickly by heaping spoonfuls as we sit on the front porch steps.

For nearly as long as I can remember, summers have also meant horses. The longer evenings provide extra hours for leisurely rides. Sometimes on afternoons when the temperature hangs sullenly in the nineties, we ride bareback down to the lake and cool off with a swim.

Recently I met up with a friend for a ride and a chat. As we saddled up, the first fat raindrops splattered the grass, but we went ahead with our plans. We had barely crossed the first field when the rain increased substantially.

"Do we keep going?" I asked.

Her reply was an enthusiastic "Yes!"

We ended up as thoroughly drenched as if we had both taken showers; yet there was something exhilarating about riding down a muddy road, laughing as the warm rain streamed down our faces. We had once agreed that there is a fundamental unfairness about life, in that when you are young enough not to have to work and be "responsible," you are not old enough to appreciate it. Then you grow up, and suddenly there is never enough time to enjoy the simple pleasures once taken for granted. We decided that when the opportunity came along to have fun for fun's sake, we'd be wise to take advantage of it.

After the ride, we untacked and turned our equally soaked horses out to pasture and sloshed homeward.

"Doesn't this make you feel like a kid again?" my friend laughed, smiling radiantly. I could only agree.

If for only a couple of hours, we had thrown work, responsibility, worries, and everything else "adult" to the wind; and we had held in our hands the joyous freedom that is summer.

Bright Meadows

Grace Noll Crowell

I am longing for the meadows of the world.
City-surrounded, I would seek and find
Some flower-strewn, wind-swept meadow there to walk
And rest my tired heart, my troubled mind.
With the wind for my companion and a lark,
Native to meadows, trilling out his song,
Water clear and high, and the whispering grass
Revealing its secrets—I would walk for long.

Breathing the clean air, bathed in the sun's clear light,
I would be healed and cleansed of the dust of years,
There would be laughter again for my sober lips,
And my eyes again would know the relief of tears.
Meadows were made for healing, for release—
I would walk them through and find their gift of peace.

An Old Familiar Road

May Smith White

I saw the low hills stretch before my eyes,
And shadows made the road look as of old—
And when each treetop met the bluing skies
I closely watched the purple dusk unfold.
Here were the things that I had yearned to see:
A spring-fed branch that runs with hurried speed,
And cattle resting here beneath a tree;
The pattern is so like a cherished creed.

Late evening found the stars glowing bright,
The road familiar as in other years;
But then, a whippoorwhil reclaimed the night
And time stood still, erasing olden fears.
In leaving here I found my faith renewed,
Each bit of doubt grew faded and subdued.

I DO NOT TREASURE MAN-MADE THINGS

Anton J. Stoffle

I do not treasure man-made things,
Like objects owned by wealthy kings,

Nor do I seek a life of fame,
Forgetting friends in fortune's name.

The earthly gifts which money buys
Are made for fools and not the wise,

But give me mountains, lakes, and streams,
Great worlds of God to fill my dreams.

The grass of green and trees galore
Where flowers bloom forevermore;

A sky of blue and shining sun—
There let me dwell 'til life is done,

And someday when life's book shall close,
I'll be content with what I chose.

Photo Opposite
YOSEMITE FALLS
L. Burton/H. Armstrong Roberts

THROUGH MY WINDOW
Pamela Kennedy

What a wondrous thing a tree is! It is an organism that asks very little, yet continually contributes to all of nature. Behind our house is an enormous example—an aged banyan tree impressive not only for its size, but for its quiet elegance as well.

Banyans are unusual in that they have aerial roots that drop from their branches, reach the earth, take hold, and somehow—known only to God, the botanist, and the banyan—grow new trunks. It makes for a base that looks like dozens of woody pillars all tumbled and intertwined in a vertical labyrinth.

My particular banyan has a base that measures over one hundred feet in circumference and a canopy of green branches stretching one hundred and fifty feet from side to side. This one tree provides a home and playground for creatures large and small, and has presided over weddings, barbecues, adolescent love trysts, and great events in world history.

When Pearl Harbor was bombed in 1941 the banyan stood as a silent witness, just one hundred yards behind the USS *Arizona*. While the battle raged and the flashing bombs and searing smoke scorched its leaves and branches, the mighty tree watched impassively. When the ships were sunk, the airplanes gone, and the fires extinguished, the tree remained—mute and magnificent.

Today its arms bear up young climbers seeking to escape the dinner call. Boys who play at pirate ships climb high in banyan rigging to spy out distant islands, and girls find ivory towers for playing princess. No Rapunzel ever wept in deeper sorrow than these young pretenders high in their branchy prisons. They braid together drooping root fibers to create swings and hammocks for their play. Tarzans swing on dangling root vines and shout their jungle calls to imagi-

clamor. They catch up on the day's events, I suppose, glad to have their tree free from noisy children once again.

Ants and beetles bore and burrow among the leafy layers piled upon the ground. In damp coolness, they lay their eggs and fetch and carry food. Up and down the smooth gray bark they climb to secret caverns tucked between knotted roots and branches. Noiselessly they parade from limb to limb, full of secret insect plans and purposes.

And in all the activity, the tree patiently stands and waits, allowing invasions of birds and bugs and boys without complaint. Ceaselessly it puts out leathery green leaves and small red berries, sunrise after sunrise. Time means little to this old tree.

Its very existence is a comfort—and a condemnation. Its solid strength reminds me to be done with fretting and worrying. Its quiet coolness invites me to trade stress for still serenity. In its permanence I am called to remember the transience of my life and I am challenged to make the days I have a contribution.

I will not always live near this great banyan tree, but I will long recall its lessons. For in its quiet way it has taught me to appreciate the magnificence of creation. And to say once more with awe—what a wondrous thing a tree is!

Pamela Kennedy is a freelance writer of short stories, articles, essays, and children's books. Wife of a naval officer and mother of three children, she has made her home on both U.S. coasts and currently resides in Hawaii. She draws her material from her own experiences and memories, adding bits of imagination to create a story or mood.

nary predators.

But when the sun has set and the children have climbed down and run away, the birds return, chattering and squawking in incessant

Photo Overleaf
CLARETCUP CACTUS
Arizona
T. Algire/H. Armstrong Roberts

Our Beautiful Land

Bessie Trull Law

Happiness is reached in finding
Where the wind and water sing,
Where rugged trails are winding
Through a meadow to a spring;
Rushing from a snow-capped mountain,
Warbling with the passing breeze,
Rippling rhythms toward a fountain
Framed in swaying willow trees.

Far from all the crash and rumble
Of a busy city street,
With our spirits high, but humble,
While we stroll at nature's feet,
Feeling music charm and cheer us
Where the heart will understand
That a father's love is near us
In the beauty of our land.

Many Things to Me

Jaye Giammarino

You are the blessed earth beneath my feet,
The quarried cliffs, the valleys wet with dew;
You are the endless fields of yellow wheat
And corn so tall its screens the land from view.
From soil made rich with rivers running wide
Your pointed pines reach up to touch the sky;
As land of bursting harvests you provide
The food for half the world in good supply.

A nation made of fifty states, all free
That stretch three thousand miles from east
    to west
United by a trying history
From Rockies down to Allegheny's breast.
You are America and stir my soul
With love for you and resolve to keep you whole.

NATURE

Henry David Thoreau

O Nature! I do not aspire
To be the highest in thy choir—
To be a meteor in thy sky,
Or comet that may range on high;
Only a zephyr that may blow
Among the reeds by the river low;
Give me thy most privy place
Where to run my airy race.

In some withdrawn, unpublic mead
Let me sigh upon a reed,
Or in the woods, with leafy din,
Whisper the still evening in:
Some still work give me to do—
Only—be it near to you!

For I'd rather be thy child
And pupil, in the forest wild,
Than be the king of men elsewhere,
And most sovereign slave of care;
To have one moment of thy dawn,
Than share the city's year forlorn.

BITS & PIECES

The heavens and the earth alike speak of God, and the great natural world is but another Bible, which clasps and binds the written one; for nature and grace are one—grace the heart of the flower, and nature its surrounding petals.

Henry Ward Beecher

Surely there is something in the unruffled calm of nature that overawes our little anxieties and doubts; the sight of the deep blue sky, and the clustering stars above, seem to impart a quiet to the mind.

Jonathan Edwards

There is virtue in country houses, in gardens and orchards, fields, streams, and groves, in rustic recreations and plain manners, that neither cities nor universities enjoy.

Amos Bronson Alcott

The country is both the philosopher's garden and library, in which he reads and contemplates the power, wisdom, and goodness of God.

William Penn

I have learned
To look on nature, not as in the hour
Of thoughtless youth; but hearing oftentimes
The still, sad music of humanity,
Not harsh nor grating, though of
     ample power
To chasten and subdue. And I have felt
A presence that disturbs me with the joy
Of elevated thoughts: a sense sublime
Of something far more deeply interfused,
Whose dwelling is the light of setting suns,
And the round ocean and the living air,
And the blue sky, and in the mind of man.

William Wordsworth

Oh, what a glory doth this earth put on, for him who with a fervent heart goes forth under the bright and glorious sky and looks on duties well-performed and days well-spent.

Henry Wadsworth Longfellow

Nothing is rich but the inexhaustible wealth of nature. She shows us only surfaces, but she is a million fathoms deep.

Ralph Waldo Emerson

71

Mount Rushmore

Maragret Williams Stevens

Before men came,
   with rope and tool
I was one of a myriad,
But now I see through
   massive eyes,
And wisdom is my brow.

When lightning breaks
   the darkened sky,
Spilling rain,
My faces weep,
Remembering.

But at the dawning hour
When amethyst and gold fuse
In the eastern sky,
Gigantic eyes, dry with the
   coming day,
Regain their depth and clarity
And gaze with tender greatness
Across the wooded hills.

MT. RUSHMORE
South Dakota
Dietrich Stock Photos

My Country

Russell W. Davenport

America lives in her simple homes:
The weathered door, the old wisteria vine,
The dusty barnyard where the rooster roams,
The common trees like elm and oak and pine.
In furniture for comfort, not for looks,
In names like Jack and Pete and Caroline,
In neighbors you can trust and honest books,
And peace, and hope, and opportunity.

She lives like destiny in Mom, who cooks
On gleaming stoves her special fricassee
And jams and cakes and endless apple pies.
She lives in Dad, the family referee,
Absorbing Sunday news with heavy eyes;
And in the dog, and in the shouting kids
Returning home from school to memorize
The history of the ancient pyramids.

And still she lives in them when darkness wakes
The distant smells and infinite katydids,
And the valleys, like black and fearsome lakes
Guarded by windows of American light,
While in the wind the family maple rakes
The lucent stars westward across the night,
And still, however far her children go
To venture in the world beyond her sight

Those little windows shine incognito
Across incredulous humanity
That all the people of the earth may know
The embattled destination of the free:
Not peace, not rest, not pleasure—but to dare
To face the axiom of democracy:
Freedom is not to limit but to share,
And freedom here is freedom everywhere.

★

Fourth of July Celebrations

Betty W. Stoffel

Let there be prayers as well as
   great parades,
Let hymns combine with patriotic songs,
Let there be leaders of the future days,
With heroes of the past amid the throngs.
Let reverent silence punctuate the noise,
Let God be praised for this great land of ours,
Let sober meditation balance joys
And grave humility mark crucial hours.

CAPE MAY, NEW JERSEY
Superstock

Let statesmanship grow from this
    nation's need,
Let citizenship be equal to these days
That godly men who gave their
    lives indeed
Be not betrayed by dull, indifferent ways.
Let joyfulness, not wildness, mark
    the Free,
That God may find us worth our liberty!

BUILDING A NATION

Edna Jaques

It isn't battlefields and guns
    that make a nation great,
Or clanking arms or marching men
    or panoply of state.
It isn't pageantry or power
    where might and triumph ride,
For kingdoms are not built on war
    or nations fed on pride.

It's the little homes against the earth
    where peace and love abide,
It's rugged hills and quiet fields
    across the countryside.
It's children trudging off to school
    secure and clean and gay,
Who own the right to childhood,
    the right to laugh and play.

It's stony fields and little brooks
    with hidden age–old springs.
It's tender songs of youth and love
    that someone's mother sings.
It's love of home and firelight;
    it's sweat and faith and toil—
The souls of men who earn their bread
    from sun and rain and soil.

It's something deeper still than this,
    beyond our heart and ken,
A faith that sees the good that lies
    within the hearts of men.
A woman glad to bear a child
    protected by her mate.
It's home and love and family
    that make a nation great.

An *ideals* Special Edition

In honor of the brave men and women who throughout our history have fought and died so that Americans might live freely, the editors of *Ideals* have published a special commemorative edition, entitled OUR AMERICA!

Well-known American masterpieces accompany majestic words from our history. Breathtaking photographs illustrate America's most cherished symbols of freedom.

OUR AMERICA!, printed on quality paper with laminated paper cover, is the perfect gift for young and old because we have included many of our country's most historic moments—events, words, and symbols that every citizen should know.

You'll want to own and display this beautiful volume in which we have assembled words and pictures that best symbolize "America". . .

- •Declaration of Independence
- •Bill of Rights
- •"The Star Spangled Banner"
- •Gettysburg Address
- •Rockwell's "Four Freedoms" paintings
- •Iwo Jima Memorial
- •Statue of Liberty
- •President Kennedy's inaugural address
- •National Cathedral
- •Civil Rights Memorial
- •Vietnam Memorial . . . and many more!

*Supply is limited, so order your copy today.

*Single issue only $6.95 plus $2.00 postage and handling. (Order # I10990A)

*Special Offer: 5 copies with envelopes for gift presentation only $24.95 plus $3.00 postage and handling. (Order # I07653A)

Make checks payable to Ideals Publishing Corp., fill out the order form, and enclose in envelope provided. Or send orders to:

Ideals Publishing Corp.
Dept. OUR AMERICA!
P.O. Box 148000
Nashville, TN 37214-8000

For credit card orders, call toll-free: 1-800-558-4343

ideals
Celebrating Life's Most Treasured Moments